# Who is Haunting
# Hilda Hardmouth?

## Karen Wallace

## illustrated by Mike Phillips

SCHOLASTIC

*To Ingrid with love*

Scholastic Children's Books,
Commonwealth House, 1-19 New Oxford Street,
London, WC1A 1NU, UK
a division of Scholastic Ltd
London ~ New York ~ Toronto ~ Sydney ~ Auckland
Mexico City ~ New Delhi ~ Hong Kong

First published by Scholastic Ltd, 2004

Text copyright © Karen Wallace, 2004
Illustrations copyright © Mike Phillips, 2004

ISBN 0 439 96881 X

Printed and bound by AIT Nørhaven A/S, Denmark

2 4 6 8 10 9 7 5 3 1

# Chapter One

Hilda Hardmouth should never have been a teacher – let alone a headteacher – because Hilda Hardmouth hated children. She hated the way they laughed and shouted when they were happy, like now when they were on their break. She hated the way their eyes shone and their faces broke into huge grins. But most of all she hated the fact that children knew how to have a good time. Somewhere deep inside her strange mind, Hilda Hardmouth knew she had never had a good time in her life.

Hilda Hardmouth sat at her huge black desk in her dark stuffy study in her little house beside the school. She stared at a large shiny book in front of her. DISCIPLINE was stamped in sharp letters on the front. Inside, it looked like an address book with letters down the outside edge of the pages. Each of the letters stood for different rules. A – *always walk never run*. B – *balls are not allowed in school grounds*. C – *coats or jackets must be buttoned up at all times*. Hilda Hardmouth loved writing rules, and letters like D were her favourite because there were lots and lots of rules beginning with D. *Don't smile when a teacher is talking to you. Don't make stupid excuses.*

Best of all: *don't speak if at all possible.*

Hilda Hardmouth licked the stub of a pencil she clutched between her fingers. She was just about to write another rule beginning with D when something so terrible happened she almost fainted. A big ball bounced against the window of her study. She flipped back to B. *Balls are not allowed in school grounds.*

Hilda jumped up from her desk and roared like a mad bull. Indeed, she even looked like a mad bull. When she was angry, her head swung dangerously on her shoulders. She slammed the rulebook shut and rushed past her courtyard and into the playground next door.

"Who is breaking the rules?" she bellowed. "Who is kicking a ball?"

All around her children were playing and laughing. They stopped and shook their heads. "Not me, Miss Hardmouth," cried a chorus of voices.

"Liars," muttered Hilda Hardmouth to herself. She turned back to her courtyard where one hopeful-looking gnome spent all day holding a fishing rod over a small pond.

Normally, Hilda admired the gnome. He always looked tidy. He never moved. He concentrated hard all day long. In fact, the gnome was Hilda's ideal student. But now just looking at him made her cross and she flicked the back of his neck with her stubby fingers.

She was just about to head inside when the big ball bounced into the courtyard again and rolled to a stop in front of Miss Daisy Dobson, the deputy headteacher.

Hilda looked over. "Did you throw that ball?" she snapped.

"Of course not," replied Daisy Dobson patiently. Daisy Dobson was the nicest and most popular teacher in the school and she lived next door to Hilda Hardmouth. But even she was beginning to find working with Hilda impossible.

"No one ignores my rules," snarled Hilda Hardmouth. She picked up the ball and jabbed it with a pair of scissors she kept on a string around her waist.

Then she threw
it as hard as she
could at an old
oak tree in the
corner of the
courtyard.

It landed with a crumpled *thud* on the
ground. She stomped across the courtyard,
picked it up and
dropped it in
the dustbin.

Keith and Kelly Clay stood behind the hedge and smirked at each other. They were the nastiest kids in the school and everyone else hated them. Everyone, that is, except for Hilda Hardmouth, who was particularly fond of bullies.

"Nice kick, sis," said Keith. He had sharp weaselly eyes and rubbery lips.

"It's smart to make the old bag angry," replied Kelly. She was short and stocky with sharp features and a mean slit of a mouth. "Then she'll pick on someone else and we'll get the credit."

Kelly smirked. "We're so useful around the school. Didn't Miss Hardmouth say so herself?"

Keith smirked back. "She certainly did. In fact, aren't we going to be made prefects at the end of the week?"

"Yup. Then we can really run the place!"

"Come on," said Keith. "Let's get back to the classroom before the break bell goes. I want to write something rude on the blackboard and blame it on someone else." He stopped to trample on a beetle that was walking harmlessly through the grass.

Then the two of them skirted the playground where the other children were and sneaked into the school by the side door.

"What's *this*?" Hilda Hardmouth stomped back to the hollow oak tree in her courtyard. She bent down and picked up a small round bottle. It was made of rough blue glass that you couldn't see through and there was a stopper stuck in its neck. *Do Not Open* was written in spidery letters across the front.

Hilda shook the bottle. "Doesn't sound like there's anything inside," she said. "What was it doing there?"

Daisy Dobson shrugged. "It must have been knocked over when you threw the ball against the tree." She peered at the bottle. "It looks quite old."

"Old and *dirty*," snapped Hilda Hardmouth. She tossed the bottle towards the dustbin full of dead leaves and hurried inside.

Hilda didn't notice that the bottle missed the dustbin. Neither did she notice that as it fell to the ground, the stopper came out.

That night the moon hung in the sky like a big yellow plate. It shone down on the gnome still patiently fishing by the pond and it shone on the blue bottle that lay by the dustbin in the corner of the yard.

Then out of the
corner of his eye
the gnome saw
a thin plume
of smoke curl up
from beside the
dustbin and into
the cold night air.
The smoke coiled
like a snake
across the
courtyard and
slowly turned
into the most
extraordinary-
looking cat.

The gnome had seen a lot of cats in his
time but he had never seen a cat like this.
It had fur that shone like silver and teeth that
sparkled like diamonds. But, strangest of all,
its eyes were red and purple and spun like
windmills at a funfair.

It takes a lot to make a gnome speak. In fact, when the gnome thought about it later, he realized he had never spoken at all before that night. But now as he stared into the spinning red and purple eyes, he felt as if he was under a spell. Suddenly he heard a voice and it was coming from his own mouth! "Who are you?" he gasped. "Where have you come from?"

"I'm Thunderclaws," said the cat. "And I've been locked up in a bottle for almost four hundred years."

"Four hundred years!" cried the gnome. "That's impossible."

Thunderclaws' red and purple eyes spun round. "Not if you're a ghost, it isn't."

"A ghost!" gasped the gnome. He thought his knees would crumple. "You d-d-don't want to haunt me, do you?"

"I don't want anything to do with you," snarled Thunderclaws. "I want a witch. And I want one *now!*"

"A witch?" croaked the gnome. "There aren't any witches around here!"

Thunderclaws twanged the gnome's fishing rod with his tail. "Don't mess with me, gnome. There must be a witch. It's Halloween tomorrow."

"So what?" said the gnome.

"Witches fly on Halloween," growled Thunderclaws. "I need to find a witch so I can fly away for ever and not get stuck in that bottle again." He held up his paws and bared his claws. They glowed horribly in the moonlight. "And you're going to help me or I'll rip your pretty blue coat into ribbons."

Suddenly, a horrible sound floated into the night. It was a cross between the shriek of fingernails dragging over a blackboard and a bull snorting. "Detention! Black mark! Rude boy! Bad girl! Detention! Black mark! NO!"

Thunderclaws felt the fur on the back of his neck prickle in a familiar way. "What was *that?*" he asked.

"Hilda Hardmouth," muttered the gnome. "She always talks in her sleep."

"Who's Hilda Hardmouth?" asked Thunderclaws. His tail flicked from side to side. A surge of excitement rushed through his strange silver body.

"Promise you won't rip my coat?" said the gnome.

"Promise," replied Thunderclaws. "Who is she?"

"She's the headteacher at this school," said the gnome.

"You sure she's not a witch?"

"Positive." The gnome snorted. "The children might not agree, though."

Thunderclaws' red and purple eyes spun like windmills in a hurricane. "Thanks, Gnome. I owe you one."

It was late at night but Daisy Dobson couldn't sleep. It so happened that at that very moment she looked down into the courtyard from her bedroom window in the house next door to Hilda Hardmouth. Her heart banged in her chest! A truly horrible-looking silvery cat sailed into the air and disappeared through the wall of Hilda Hardmouth's bedroom!

Daisy Dobson stumbled back to her bed.
"It's a ghost! It's a ghost!" she croaked to
herself. "What am I going to do?" But as she
fell back on her pillows, she remembered
two girls who used to go to the school. They
were called Lily and Bertha and they'd set up
a business called Ghost Getters.

Daisy Dobson pulled the bedcovers over
her head and tried to stop shaking. She had
to find the Ghost Getters first thing the next
morning!

# Chapter Two

Lily Typhoon looked up from her tiny silver desk and sighed. In front of her lay a huge open book. Written at the top of each page were the words GHOST GETTERS. Underneath were two columns: JOBS DONE and JOBS TO DO. The second column went down to the bottom of the page.

"We've got so much work, I don't know where to begin," she said to her partner, Bertha Truncheon.

On the other the other side of the room, Bertha Truncheon laughed. "That's better than having no work at all!"

Bertha's desk was made of three planks laid across two oil drums. She never kept a book with a list. All her appointments were scrawled in biro on the wooden planks.

In many ways, the two partners in Ghost Getters could not have been more different. Lily Typhoon was small and silvery with black, almond-shaped eyes. Bertha had red, curly hair and two green eyes that twinkled in her round face. She was also strong and particularly good at wrestling.

This was because Bertha looked after the jobs that involved tough, heavy-duty ghosts – the kind that hid under concrete building foundations or haunted wrecking balls. Lily, on the other hand, took care of the gentler kind of ghost – like delicate princesses who swept through castle walls in gauzy ballgowns, or see-through unicorns that leapt over fountains in the middle of velvety lawns. It was a perfect partnership and they were both good at what they did. Indeed, from the moment they had left Ghost Hunting School and set up Ghost Getters, they had never been short of jobs.

"Don't worry, Lily," cried Bertha. "We'll begin at the beginning like we always do and work our way through to the end." She banged her meaty fist down on her desk and made the planks jump. "Now, what's my next job?" She peered at the scrawls all over her desk. "I can't find it."

"The fire hose at the London Zoo."

Bertha drew her brows together. "The one that's haunted by that poor old elephant?"

"Exactly. The zoo manager is getting very upset," said Lily.

Bertha laughed. "You mean his visitors are getting very wet."

"Something like that." Lily grinned. "Apparently he heard the hose make a trumpeting sound last night just like an elephant."

"I'm on my way." Bertha jumped out of her chair just as the specially made creaky oak door opened and Daisy Dobson staggered into the room, looking very worried.

"Miss Dobson," cried Lily. She looked at Bertha. "Goodness me! We haven't seen you since we left school."

Bertha looked at the teacher's white, shaking face. "What on earth is the matter?"

Daisy Dobson took a deep breath and started talking.

Twenty minutes later, Lily Typhoon looked up from her notebook. "So after you saw the silver cat disappear through the wall, you heard meowing?"

"And cackling," whispered Daisy Dobson. "Terrible cackling."

"So then what did you do?" asked Bertha.

"I was going to get the
funny blue bottle from
the dustbin but –"
Daisy Dobson buried
her face in her hands –
"I couldn't. I was
too frightened."

"Don't you worry, Miss Dobson," said
Bertha, kindly. "We'll look after things now."

Lily led her to the door. "Go home. Have a
nice cup of tea and leave it to the Ghost
Getters." She opened the heavy oak door
and helped Daisy Dobson up the stairs.

When she came back down, Bertha was
standing still as a statue looking at the office
calendar. "Lily!" she said in a hollow voice.
"It's Halloween tonight!"

Lily understood immediately. "Halloween
and a ghost cat is on the loose!"

Bertha nodded. "And if you were a ghost
cat, what would you want for Halloween?"

"My very own witch," said Lily slowly.

"Exactly!" cried Bertha. "Quick! We've got to find that bottle and save Hilda Hardmouth before it's too late!"

Inside Hilda Hardmouth's house, the noises were just as Daisy Dobson had described them. A yowling, howling meow sound mixed with high-pitched cackling. Lily and Bertha looked at each other. The only strange thing about the cackling was that it sounded happy, and not at all mean or nasty.

"I think we'd better have a closer look," muttered Bertha.

Lily nodded and they crept up to the front window.

HOOOWWLL~
MEEEOOWW~

They couldn't believe what they saw!

Hilda Hardmouth was riding round and round her dining room on a floor polisher. A dustbin bag was tied around her neck like a cloak and she was grinning and hooting with laughter. A large silver cat was sitting on her shoulders and he seemed to be whispering in her ear.

Bertha and Lily were amazed. Everyone knew that Hilda Hardmouth never grinned, let alone laughed. The Ghost Getters felt the skin prickle all over their bodies. They looked again at the extraordinary cat on Hilda's shoulders – it was definitely a ghost! There was no doubt about it. And it had something to do with Hilda's odd behaviour.

"Come on," whispered Lily. "Let's get that bottle and get out of here before that cat senses us!"

Bertha nodded and they bent double and crept around the side of the house into the courtyard.

There in the corner, just as Daisy Dobson had described, was the dustbin. Lily and Bertha ran up to it.

"Did you bring the ghostometer?" asked Lily.

Bertha nodded and peered into the dustbin. But there was no bottle. She rooted around in the leaves trying to find it. "It's not here," she said to Lily.

But Lily had spotted something glinting in the sunlight next to the dustbin. It was the blue bottle.

"Wait, I see it," she told Bertha, and pointed to the ground.

Bertha picked up the bottle and looked at the label with the old-fashioned spidery writing. *Do Not Open.*

"There's the stopper, too," whispered Lily. "It must have fallen out when Miss Hardmouth threw the bottle."

Bertha nodded slowly. "That's how the ghost cat escaped."

Bertha unzipped the ghostometer from her backpack and pointed it at the small glass bottle. She flicked on the switch. Lights flashed and a needle wiggled on a dial. There were three sections on the dial. Yellow for NOT HAUNTED. Orange for HAUNTED. Red for HORRIBLY HAUNTED. The needle swung over to red as far as it could go!

Thunderclaws sat in the upstairs window and watched as Bertha and Lily stared at the ghostometer.

Their voices floated up into the air.

"We've got to stop him before he turns her into a witch," said Lily in a low voice.

"And get him back into this bottle," said Bertha.

"But how?" asked Lily.

Bertha narrowed her eyes. "It's Halloween tonight. He's running out of time. Let's follow them and see what he gets up to!"

"Good plan!"

From the upstairs window, Thunderclaws growled a terrible ghostly growl and his red and purple eyes spun round. No one was going to lock him back up in a bottle again. He flew downstairs and sank his claws into Hilda Hardmouth's shoulders.

"Oooh pussykins," cooed Hilda Hardmouth. "I was wondering where you were!"

Thunderclaws rubbed his silver face against her ear and purred. And as he purred he sent the strangest thoughts into Hilda Hardmouth's head. Suddenly she wanted to go shopping and she knew exactly what she had to get.

"Oooh pussykins," cooed Hilda Hardmouth, as she picked up a large wicker basket. "What lovely ideas you have! I wish I'd met you years ago!"

Thunderclaws arched his back and purred even louder. Things with Hilda were going very nicely. Very nicely indeed. He just had to make sure that no one interfered with his plans.

The Ghost Getters weren't the only ones who were visiting Hilda Hardmouth that Saturday morning. Behind the dustbins alongside Hilda Hardmouth's house, Keith and Kelly Clay exchanged worried glances. They were good at spying on people and usually they got the results they wanted. They had already spent a lot of time spying on Hilda Hardmouth before getting thrown out of their old school because it seemed to them that Hilda was just the sort of person they could get on with. And sure enough, everything had worked out perfectly.

Until now.

Hilda Hardmouth had changed. She wasn't horrible to everyone she saw. She didn't say unkind things just for the fun of it and, worst of all, she had stopped yelling and scowling all the time.

"There's something funny going on in there, Keith," muttered Kelly. "She's turning nice and we don't want that."

"Too right," said Keith. "We picked Hilda Hardmouth because she was a nasty old bag. If she turns nice she'll throw us out. Nice people always do."

Kelly nodded. "If we change schools some dumb teacher will try and make us do some work again."

Keith stuck out his lip and shook his head. "I ain't working."

"So what are we going to do?" Kelly said.

Keith narrowed his eyes and looked thoughtful. "Follow her and see what happens!" he said.

# Chapter Three

"Look here, Miss Hardmouth," said Mr Tug the dentist. "Are you sure about this? I won't be able to put them back, you know."

"All right. I'll keep four." There was a terrible cackling sound as Hilda Hardmouth burst out laughing and the cat on her shoulder meowed *horribly*. It was almost as if it was laughing too. Mr Tug was just about to insist that the cat be removed when he found himself staring into a pair of spinning red and purple eyes.

"Yes, of course," muttered Mr Tug to the cat. Even though he knew it was crazy to talk to a cat. "I'll do exactly what she wants." He picked up his drill and leant forwards.

In the waiting room, Bertha Truncheon and Lily Typhoon examined the contents of Hilda Hardmouth's basket. There was a pumpkin, a dozen dried frogs and a tube of lizard paste in the basket. There was even an old-fashioned iron cauldron and a huge wooden spoon. And at the very bottom was a packet of little white pills.

"Bertha," said Lily slowly. "What if Miss Hardmouth really wants to be a witch?"

Bertha looked thoughtful. "I see what you mean. Of course it's the cat that's behind it all, but she did look really happy."

Lily nodded. "She must have kissed that cat a hundred times!" She looked around the dentist's surgery and shuddered at the pictures of teeth on the wall. "But why would she want to go to the dentist?"

Bertha raised her eyebrows. "It's something to do with that cat."

"I wonder what these are for." Lily picked up the packet of little white pills and was just about to read the instructions when Keith and Kelly Clay burst into the room. Lily quickly put the pills into her pocket.

"What you doing following our headteacher around?" snarled Keith. "You leave her alone."

Bertha stood up to her full size and her green eyes glittered angrily. "And just who, exactly, are you?"

"We're Keith and Kelly Clay." Keith puffed himself up like a toad. "We're Miss Hardmouth's new prefects."

"Not yet, we're not," hissed Kelly.

"Shaddup!" snapped Keith.

"And what is your reason for following Miss Hardmouth?" asked Lily in a thin, icy voice.

Keith tried another tactic. It was difficult but it might work. "We're worried about her," he said in the most worried voice he could manage. "Ever since yesterday, she's changed and we think she should see a doctor or something to change her back again."

Bertha narrowed her eyes. "I think you two should go home and leave this to us. We're professionals and we know what we're doing."

"And I think you're a pair of no-good busybodies and you should mind your own business!" shouted Kelly, losing her temper.

"We've spent a lot of time getting old Hardmouth on our side and we're not going to let her go all soppy now."

Lily was stunned. She had never met such a pair of nasty kids in her life. She decided to lead them on and see what she could find out. "So you two run the school, right?"

"Yeah," said Keith, falling for the compliment. "We're Miss Hardmouth's favourites." He paused and his face twisted with rage. "Until that disgusting animal showed up. Now all she does is talk to her cat!"

At that moment, the dentist's door swung open and Hilda Hardmouth stamped into the room with a great big smile on her face. It was a weird, witchy-looking smile because she had two teeth in the bottom of her mouth and two teeth at the top.

"Bertha! Lily!" cried Hilda Hardmouth. "How lovely to see you!" She looked sideways and chuckled. "And this is my beautiful pussycat! I love him to bits!"

Bertha and Lily found themselves staring into Thunderclaws' red and purple eyes. And to their amazement, instead of an angry howling, they heard a plaintive mewing in their heads. *Please leave us alone. She's happy and I'm happy. What's wrong with that?*

But before Bertha and Lily had time to think. Keith suddenly jumped at Thunderclaws and tried to knock him from Hilda Hardmouth's shoulders.

"How dare you come near me or my cat?" bellowed Hilda Hardmouth. "Who do you think you are?"

"Miss Hardmouth," shouted Kelly desperately. "It's us! Keith and Kelly Clay. We're your prefects. We're trying to help you!"

Thunderclaws put his face to Hilda Hardmouth's ear.

"I don't like brats!" snapped Hilda Hardmouth. She picked up her basket, jumped on her broom and galloped out of the door.

"This is trouble," said Keith to Kelly. "Big trouble."

"Why don't you go home, where you belong?" said Bertha firmly. "We'll sort things out."

"Shaddup!" screamed Kelly. "We'll do what we want!" Then they stuck out their tongues and ran out of the door.

Bertha looked at Lily. "We must talk to Daisy Dobson."

Lily nodded. "Maybe Hilda would be happier as a witch."

"Exactly," said Bertha and they set off back to the Ghost Getters' office as fast as they could.

# Chapter Four

Miss Dobson was waiting outside the Ghost Getters' office door. "I'm sorry to disturb you again," she said quickly. "It's just that I've been so worried about Hilda and I've been thinking—"

"So have we," said Bertha quickly. "Let's talk inside."

They went into the office and Lily made everyone tea. "First things first," she said as she put the cups on the table. "Tell us about the Clay twins."

Half an hour and six cups of tea later, the Ghost Getters had thought up a plan.

"I know this is going to sound strange," said Bertha slowly. "But Lily and I think Hilda Hardmouth really wants to turn into a witch."

Lily nodded and held up the packet of white pills she had taken from Hilda Hardmouth's basket. "These are flying-sickness pills. I'm almost positive that that's exactly what she wants to do tonight."

Daisy Dobson swallowed. "You mean she wants to fly off as a witch and never come back?"

Bertha nodded. "And that's what the ghostly cat wants, too. He needs to find a witch in time for Halloween."

"You see, not *all* ghosts are bad," explained Lily. "And this cat might be one of that kind."

Daisy Dobson nodded slowly. "I think I do. Certainly, there's no denying the fact that Hilda is happier now than I've ever seen her – even if she is being haunted." She sighed. "And apart from anything else, she's just not a good headteacher."

"She can't be if she made those terrible twins prefects," said Bertha, grimly.

"So what is the best thing we can do?" asked Daisy Dobson.

Bertha stood up. A huge moon was rising outside the office window. "I think we should go to Hilda Hardmouth's house. Then if we have to make a move, we can do it quickly."

"How can I help?" asked Daisy Dobson. "I want Hilda to be happy even if that means she turns into a witch."

"Then the best thing you can do is keep an eye on those dreadful Clay twins," said Lily. "If anyone is going to cause trouble, it will be them."

Bertha jumped up and rummaged in the cupboard. A moment later, she pulled out something that looked like a hand-held Hoover.

Lily stared at her. "Why are you taking the Ghost Hoover with you?"

Bertha smiled. "Bargaining power."

Thunderclaws knew the Ghost Getters were standing on Hilda Hardmouth's doorstep and he knew he had to make a decision. It was so difficult to guess human beings' behaviour. Gnomes were easier. Nevertheless, he had a feeling that the Ghost Getters understood what he was doing and why. After all, anyone who had studied the bottle and knew about ghosts would have put two and two together, and they could see that his new witch was happy. But he was still going to need their help, so he decided to be as friendly as he possibly could.

The truth was that Thunderclaws had grown rather fond of Hilda Hardmouth. To begin with she had just been the first witch he could find in a hurry. And it wasn't even as if she had the makings of a good one. Hilda Hardmouth couldn't even ride a bicycle. She was one of the clumsiest humans he had ever met. He knew that teaching her to fly was going to be difficult. Even so, there was something about Hilda that made Thunderclaws care, and he hadn't cared about anything except himself for four hundred years.

So when Hilda Hardmouth opened her front door and led Lily and Bertha into her little courtyard, Thunderclaws tried to appear as friendly as possible and used all his ghostly powers so they could read each other's minds.

The Ghost Getters looked at the cauldron positioned above a roaring bonfire and turned towards Thunderclaws. He turned his tail into a question mark.

*What do you think of my new witch?*

Bertha's green eyes gleamed.
*The perfect choice.*
Lily's black eyes gleamed.
*Are you going to look after her?*
Thunderclaws grinned.

*A witch's cat always looks after his witch.*
He rubbed his silvery face against her ear.
*We need each other and, besides, I've
grown rather fond of her.*

Bertha took out the Ghost Hoover.
*Are you SURE we can trust you?*
Even though Thunderclaws had been
stuck in a bottle for four hundred years,
he still recognized a ghost sucker-upper.
He knew perfectly well that with one flick of
a switch, he'd be back where he started.

Suddenly his whole body went rigid and he
let out a terrible yowl.

*Please! Please!*
*You have to*
*trust me!*

"Poor pussycat!" cried Hilda Hardmouth.
She chucked the last handful of dried frogs
into the bubbling cauldron and finished off
the tube of lizard paste.

Then she cradled Thunderclaws in her arms.
"Whatever is the matter?"
Bertha looked at Lily.
*We can trust him.*

Suddenly there was a squeal of tyres as a
car braked hard on the road outside. Daisy
Dobson burst into the courtyard.
"The Clay twins
are coming!"
she shouted.
"They've
called the fire
department!"
   "What on earth
for?" cried Lily.

Daisy Dobson swallowed. "They said a dangerous lunatic was building a huge fire in her back garden. Hilda! They want to lock you up!"

Hilda Hardmouth looked astounded. "Why me?"

"So you can be turned back into a headteacher," said Daisy Dobson.

"But I don't want to be a headteacher again!" wailed Hilda Hardmouth. "I want to be a witch! I'm happy as a witch!"

She grabbed Daisy Dobson by the hand. "You should be headteacher, Daisy."

"But how can I be headteacher?" cried Daisy.

"Easy," shouted Hilda. She threw back her head and bellowed as loud as she could. *"I RESIGN!"*

The sound of a fire engine grew louder and louder.

"What am I going to do?" wailed Hilda Hardmouth.

Thunderclaws sank his claws into her arm. There was no time to lose. They had to escape!

# Chapter Five

A car door slammed. The ugly howl of the Clay twins' voices filled the air. "This way, officers! And get the cat! He's dangerous, too!"

Thunderclaws stared desperately at the Ghost Getters as they heard the firemen begin hammering at the door. *Help me teach her to fly!*

Neither Lily nor Bertha had ever taught
a witch to fly, but in the panic, they did
the first thing that came into their minds.

Lily picked up Hilda Hardmouth's yellow
plastic broom and put it in her hands.

"Think *witch*," commanded Bertha.

Meanwhile Thunderclaws opened his
mouth and hissed as loud as he could.

"He's thinking *witch*, too!" cried Lily.
"Try, Miss Hardmouth! Try!"

Hilda Hardmouth squeezed her eyes shut and thought *witch* as hard as she could. Very, very slowly, she rose over the courtyard.

Thunderclaws was just about to leap up beside her when there was a loud *phut* and Hilda Hardmouth fell back to the ground.

A big white cloud was heading towards the moon. Thunderclaws' fur stood on end and he let out a terrible yowl. A new witch can only take off when the moon is shining full and bright!

The Clay twins and the firemen had managed to break down the front door.

It was now or never!

Out of the corner of her eye, Lily saw a broom made of twigs leaning against the dustbin. "That's the problem!" she shouted. "Plastic brooms don't work!"

Bertha shoved the broom into Hilda's hands. Thunderclaws leapt on to her shoulder.

"Think *witch*!" cried Lily again.

Thunderclaws growled! Hilda Hardmouth squeezed her eyes shut!

Keith Clay came running into the courtyard and lunged at Hilda Hardmouth with a huge fishing net in his hand. "You won't get away from me," he snarled. Beside him, Kelly tried to hook Hilda's skirt with a garden fork.

The firemen ran around the corner dragging a huge hose. "Where's the fire?" shouted one.

"Forget the fire!" screamed Kelly. "Aim that hose at her!"

But it was too late! Hilda Hardmouth
soared into the night just as the cloud passed
over the moon.

"Wow!" muttered a young fireman. "It's just
like in the movies."

"Never mind the movies!" bellowed the
Chief Fire Officer. "There is no dangerous
fire here! Where are those meddling kids
who called out the Fire Department?"

"Here!" said Bertha Truncheon. And she
gripped the Clay twins firmly by the
shoulders and dragged them across the
courtyard.

"It was all Keith's fault!" squealed Kelly.

"Liar!" screamed Keith. "It was your idea!"
He bent his head and tried to bite Bertha's
arm. "You let go! You can't boss me. You're
not headteacher."

"No, she's not!" said a firm, angry voice. Daisy Dobson strode across the courtyard and fixed the Clay twins with a terrifying glare. "I am. Miss Hardmouth has gone, and she won't be coming back!" She turned to the Chief Fire Officer. "Take them home. They won't be coming back to my school!"

The next morning, Lily Typhoon sat at her tiny silver desk in the Ghost Getters' office and flipped open the appointments book.

Bertha looked up from her own desk. "What's on today?"

"You're going to the zoo to sort out that haunted hose and I'm off to the toy shop to stop their ghost train tooting all day."

There was a knock on the door and a messenger walked in with a huge bunch of black and orange tiger lilies. There were so many of them, all anyone could see was a pair of feet.

Bertha opened the little envelope that was pinned to the wrapping paper and showed the card inside it to Lily.

To the Ghost Getters!
A thousand thanks!
You made Hilda happy and saved the school.
Daisy Dobson.

Lily smiled. "Do you think Hilda Hardmouth will ever come back?"

"Who's to say?" replied Bertha." Maybe she'll make a flying visit this time next year!"

Lily rolled her eyes and they both burst out laughing.

Look out for more spooky stories
about the Ghost Getters...

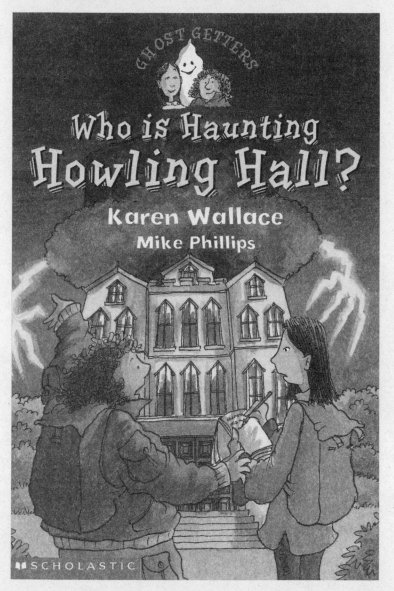

## Meet Airy Fairy.

Her wand is all wonky, her wings
are covered in sticking plaster
and her spells are always a muddle!
But she's the cutest fairy around!

Look out for this
sparkly new series...

Margaret Ryan

**Airy Fairy**

Magic Mischief!

How can one little
fairy get into such
BIG trouble?

SCHOLASTIC

Margaret Ryan

# Airy Fairy

## Magic Mess!

How can one little
fairy get into such
BIG trouble?

SCHOLASTIC